I0640568

Lord de Tabley

Poems Dramatic and Lyrical

Second Series

Lord de Tabley

Poems Dramatic and Lyrical
Second Series

ISBN/EAN: 9783744787376

Printed in Europe, USA, Canada, Australia, Japan

Cover: Foto ©Andreas Hilbeck / pixelio.de

More available books at **www.hansebooks.com**

Uniform with this in Size and Binding

POEMS, DRAMATIC AND LYRICAL.
First Series. By Lord De Tabley.
With Etched Illustrations by C. S.
Ricketts. Crown 8vo. 7s. 6d. net.
[*Second Edition.*

Of this edition 550 copies have been printed for England

POEMS

DRAMATIC AND LYRICAL : By LORD DE TABLEY

SECOND SERIES

LONDON : JOHN LANE, *at the Sign of the* BODLEY HEAD *in Vigo Street*
NEW YORK : MACMILLAN *and* COMPANY

M DCCC XCV

PREFATORY NOTE

WITH the exception of *Orpheus in Hades*, nothing in this volume has ever been printed or published before. *Orpheus* appeared in *The Nineteenth Century* of November 1893, and the poem is now reprinted with the kind permission of Mr. James Knowles, the editor of that Review.

CONTENTS

vii

CONTENTS

AN INVOCATION

An invocation for the queenly one,
  The ruler of my days and my desire :
A burning incense to my radiant sun,
  A music mounting in a shaft of fire :

An adoration and a sacrifice,
  An aureole outrayed upon her brow,
As in a silver saint of Paradise :
  A pearly necklace round a throat of snow—

Turn not the splendour of thine eyes aside,
    Though night and all her shadows are
      deceased ;
Thy glance is as the morning's to divide
  The pillared chambers of the glowing east.

A   I

The clear blue heaven returns in all my
    soul
  Dim cloud and dense forebodings haste away:
I fear no hidden rock, no ragged shoal,
    I ride at anchor in a glassy bay.

My life is as a wood, where owls and jays
    Hoot in the heavy boughs, and magpies
    rail,
Till I am weary.   Then, beyond all praise,
    I hear thy rapture, O my nightingale.

My life is as a lonely woodland mere,
    Whose sullen waters without sun repose :
And thou one ivory lily floating here,
    Marble and white, flushed with a hint of
    rose.

Thou art the silence of a mighty sea,
    Thou art the tempest cleaving night with fire:
Thou art the fragrance of all spring to me,—
    Mine, fated mine, as mine in my desire.

Before the world was builded, thou wert
    mine,
    Before the seas were laid, Fate drew thee
      dumb
Out of the void abyss: my soul to thine,
    Thro' myriad leagues of awful space has
      come.—

Swing up the golden censer, acolyte,
    Let fumes of stately frankincense arise,
As Pæan to my beautiful Delight,
    And mingle cloud-like with the cloudy skies.

I breathe but in thy breath; and, this with-
    drawn,
    My swan-like music dies upon its wing:
But smile upon me like incarnate Dawn,
    And then this Memnon, mute before, can
      sing.

THE SPIRIT OF EVEN

GENTLE Queen, that dost control
   Kingdoms pale of faded light :
Spheréd star, that ridest sole
   In between the day and night.
Silver-pulsing, planet queen,
Wrapt in robes of twilight sheen.

Loose the ox and lengthen shadows :
   Hive again the roving bee :
Still the lark o'er emerald meadows :
   Bring the fishers home from sea :
Spirit of the Eve unseen,
Shed thy influence, twilight Queen.

4

Shepherd, pipe thy plaintive lays,
   Crown her brows with radiant mist:
On her throne of purple rays
   Seat her like an amethyst:
Beaming glow-worm, amber-green,
Fair and lovely twilight Queen.

Smite, O smite the chorded lyre,
   All things praise her peaceful sway.
Poet, wake thy heart of fire,
   Ere her beauty waste away,
Pass unsung and fade unseen, '
' Pearl of Even, twilight Queen.

ODE TO FORTUNE

DEMON or goddess, who dost sway
　　The changes of our mortal state :
Before whose footstep fades away,
　　As snow, the grandeur of the great.

To some thou bringest health and fame,
　　A happy love, a faithful friend,
To some the dungeon-doors of shame,
　　Gibbet and rope, a felon's end.

Thou art almighty in thy might,
　　Heaven fades before thy fiery breath.
The giant planets of the night
　　Fall, if thy hand decree their death.

6

Wisdom is but a little child,
  Before the breath of thy command :
And Virtue, broken and beguiled,
  Rests in the hollow of thy hand.

O'er heaven and ocean, crag and vale,
  Thou waftest thy triumphant wings ;
Thou soarest on the golden gale
  With incense from an hundred springs.

Thou canst unlock the secret deep,
  And rend aside the mountain range;
And, as the spheres thro' ether sweep,
  Thou rollest round thy orb of change.

No bourn, no limit of delay,
  No rest thy alternations know ;
We quail before thy dreadful way,
  And at thy thunder step bend low.

7

Thy deep eyes search the years unborn,
　　And mock the present with disdain ;
And measure with a smile of scorn
　　Each sceptred tyrant's fleeting reign.

How brief a record can they save,
　　If only in some marble bust
Survive those features, which the grave
　　Has crumbled to a pinch of dust.

And these white ashes of an urn
　　Once made a chidden world afraid ;
But Queens to common dust return,
　　And Kings of glory quickly fade.

So when proud Egypt in her fleet
　　Beat up, with canvas all unfurled,
Inflamed with Mareotic heat,
　　To wreck the realm and clutch the world :

8

Drunk with the wine of prosperous hours,
    Insane to hope the wildest good,
She, queenly crowned with lotus flowers,
    Swept silken-sailed across the flood:

Came with musquito nets, and came
    With eunuchs, a decrepit band,
While, doting at her apron, tame
    The great triumvir gave command.

But when she saw her burning ships,
    And heard the roaring of the fire,
The wanton paled her painted lips,
    And fled the falcon Cæsar's ire.

The destiny of Rome, of man,
    Hung trembling on that awful day,
The ages and their coming plan
    Were mapped in that Ambracian bay.

9

There, Fortune, calm on Actian height,
    Above the hurtling prows and sails,
Sat arbitress to watch the fight,
    And weigh the world in battle scales.

And, when the haughty Rome was done,
    She rolled her Goths in thunder down,
Thro' ice-blue vales she called the Hun,
    She gave him Cæsar's empty crown.

Dread Deity, supremely fair,
    Daughter of heaven, serenely strong,
Smile on us, firstborn of despair,
    Give respite to our ancient wrong.

The nations narrow and expand,
    As tides that ebb, or tides that flow.
Their bounds and borders fear thy hand;
    It rears them high or wrecks them low.

10

·

All men thy intercession crave;
   The happy lovers newly wed,
The widow bending o'er a grave,
   The mother o'er a cradled head.

They perish as a robe outworn,
   As faded leaves they float away:
But in the prime where thou wert born,
   A hundred years are but a day.

Thou scatterest them like shade or sleep,
   Thou slayest them and they are slain:
Anon, thou callest o'er the deep,
   'Children of silence, come again.'

As oxen that to slaughter reel,
   Thou drivest nations with thy goad;
They are as flies upon thy wheel,
   They are as pebbles in thy road:

As emmets, who have lost their way,
　　Between the ant-hill and the sheaf:
As coral insects in a bay,
　　That weave their little inch of reef :

We last but while the day is new ;
　　The thirsty sunbeam dries us up.
Have mercy ! we are drops of dew
　　Shed for a moment in thy cup.

ORPHEUS IN HADES

ORPHEUS, HAVING DESCENDED TO THE NETHER WORLD IN
SEARCH OF EURYDICE, THUS ADDRESSES PROSERPINE

RULER and regent, to whose dread domain
The mighty flood of life and human woe
Sends down the immeasurable drift of souls,
As silted sands are rolled to Neptune's deep,
I, even I, approach your awful realms,
Queen of oblivion, lady of Acheron,
To crave one captive. I alive descend,
A live man nourished still on human bread,
A man with limbs of flesh and veins of blood,
What right have I to tread the cheerless
    field
Of the eternal exile? What despair
Hath made me undertake so dire a road;

13

A chasm, in whose mouth the tumbled
    crags,
Tumbled and jumbled, as in Titan wars,
Lie fragmented in horror, block on block,
Torn and enormous boulders. On through
    these
Undaunted down I went. I wished to die.
I held my poor life cheaply in one hand,
Cheaply and loosely, as a fluttering bird,
Whom any onward step may grant escape ;
And, at the base of the abyss, behold,
A level platform and an unknown land.
And at this point the ghostly realm begins,
And I had done with light and done with
    men,
And the sweet sun was quenched and far away.

Soon, soon I saw the spectral vanguard come,
Coasting along, as swallows, beating low
Before a hint of rain. In buoyant air,
Circling they poise, and hardly move the wing,
And rather float than fly. Then other spirits,

Shrill and more fierce, came wailing down the
  gale ;
As plaintive plovers come with swoop and
  scream
To lure our footsteps from their furrowy nest,
So these, as lapwing guardians, sailed and
  swung
To save the secrets of their gloomy lair,
And waved me back, impeding my advance.
Yet I persisted, tho' my veins ran cold
To catch the winnowing of their awful wings,
And feel the sweat-drops of their ghostly
  flight
Drip on my neck and shoulder from above,
As ice-flakes from the mantle of some cloud
That overpasses, bearing in its breast
A core of thunder and the seeds of hail.
Ye spectral bats, with latticed cobweb sails,
Shall I, around whose cradle Muses sang,
Quail at your emanations weak as rain ?
As mist I cleave your ineffectual files,
Love shall not shudder at your goblin eyes.

15

Yet have I weathered direr dread than these,
In winding from the frontier of thy realm,
Here to thy throne-step and thy sceptred
    seat,
A piteous interval, a roadway grim,
And avenued with horrors ; thick as when
The Arcadian peasant plants the frequent
    stem
Of rough-leaved, bramble-fruited mulberries,
Ranked on the causeways of the dusty roads
To feed the worm who weaves the stoles of
    queens.

Thus on each hand has peril fringed my path,
Under the strong wing of the rose-wreathed
    god :
Peril of waters, peril of the dunes,
The marsh, the fog, the whirlwind, and the
    fire,
Malignant shores with reason-blasting sights,
And the dim dungeons of the eternal curse
I traversed, and in arduous passage scaled.

Love, orbed in iris halo, step by step,
Went with me, mighty Love, who tunes my
     lyre :
Unseen he went, and breathed into my ear
The consolations of his nectared lips,
And on the utter edge of horror gave
A whisper from the fair Thessalian fields,
A hint of rosebuds ripe in crystal dew,
And the clear morning summits, poised
     above
The belt of vineyards and the zone of pines.

I, fed with vision, held securely on,
Nor heeded half the execrable sights
Which ripen in the forest of despair :
The thorn-encircled stem of human woe,
The leaves of agony's expanded rose
With glowing petals and a fiery heart.

Under the shelter of my master's plumes,
I did not turn my feet from any dread,
I took the woes full-breasted as they came ;

Then suddenly the dolorous thicket ceased,
And all the wailing of its woods retired,
Like voices of some dreadful nightingale.
And at my feet a turbid river came.

I knew the stream, I knew the flaccid roll
Of those accursed waves : sighing it ran.
Lethe thou art and worthy of thy name.
Will Love sustain me through this bitter
    flood,
Where all things are forgot ?   Maybe these
    waves
Will wash away my sorrow.   On, faint
    heart,
And bear me up, sweet Love, and guide me
    through.
And out I waded through the curdled wave
To the mid-channel : girdle-deep it grew.
Loathing I went, from waist to knee in wave,
From knee to heel in slime ; I moved as
    one
In heavy chains advancing to his doom.

But Eros found a ford and pushed me
    through ;
And whispered, 'Fear not—see, it shallows
    now.'
And when I found the hateful waves sub-
    side,
And saw the nearness of the further shore,
My heart rejoiced.   I cared not for the
    slime :
Nor those Lethean reaches daunted then,
Not the long withered reed-beds, sad in
    ooze,
Not the black bulrush bank, against whose
    stems
The lap and washing of the sequent waves
Sough on for ever.   Not the broken brows,
Steep at the river turn and undermined,
Wherefrom the snags of oak and tortured
    boughs
Project, and latticed ribs in skeleton
Jut from the crumbling margin, hung with
    weeds,

19

Trophies and wrecks of some old deluge
    gone,
That rot and fester in the eddying creeks.

Evading then these foul and crumbling
    brinks,
I planted footstep on a firmer soil.
Before me rose a great and gloomy plain,
Ridged into tracks by mighty chariot wheels,
And at its verge a formidable gate
With castled bastions like a mountain wall,
And adamantine portals smooth as ice.
And trembling I approached these Titan doors.

Then through the gate I entered Acheron,
Region of sorrow, citadel of pain,
The city with the sad-eyed citizens.
Coasts of remorse and colonies of sin
I traversed, sore of foot and sick of soul :
I saw the awful many-sided face
Of human agony.   I found the dregs
Of anguish and the deepest deeps of woe.

The bitter road is run.   The goal is gained.
Here at thy throne my gloomy journey ends,
O purple-mantled Queen, with slow grave
    eyes,
And I unbind my sandals, stained in blood,
And make petition on adorant knee.
Forgive and grant me pardon that I come.
For great is Love, who gave me pilotage,
And mighty in the land without a rose.
I come not as Alcides, sheathed in mail.
I have no shield but music and a lyre,
Seven piteous chords, strung on a tortoise
    back.
Dare I approach the impenetrable doors,
Or batter at the famished gates of hell,
So feebly furnished for the dire assault ?

Can music build the stars or mould the moon,
Or wring assent from Hades' doubtful brows ?
Can I make weep the stern and lovely Queen,
Before whose feet the ripples of the dead
Pass like an endless sea, beating her throne ?

They move her not.   In autumn's gusty
    hour
Shall the innumerable broken leaves,
The aimless russet-sided rushing leaves,
Gain pity from the hatchet-handed boor,
Who shears the stubborn oak, an eagle's
    throne?
Doth pity sting the rugged fisher folk
For the blue tunnies snared inside their net?
She will not hearken.   I shall sing in vain.

Yet song is great.   These pale dishevelled
    ghosts
Crowd in to hear with dim pathetic eyes,
And quivering corners of their charnel lips.
They rustle in from all the coasts of hell,
As starlings mustering on their evening tree,
Some blasted oak full in the sunset's eye.
And over all the mead the vibrating
Hiss of their chatter deepens.   I can move
These bat-like spectres.   Can I move their
    Queen?

Yet song is great : and in the listed war
The hero, while some martial pæan thrills,
Breathes out his soul upon the hostile spears,
And gains—a wreath to bind his temples
    dead !

Ay, song is great, and even an iron Queen,
Stern as her flinty judgment-seat of doom,
May see on music's golden plume arise
Ambrosial glimpses of a dawn divine,
And pearl-drops in the rose-red heaven of
    youth.

THE INVOCATION

Queen, thou shalt hearken by the breath and
    fragrance
Of those old lawns at Enna : by the gales
That woke the drooping sister-violets,
And mingled all the sward with musky
    thyme :
By the trembling iris, by the speckled eye-
    bright,

By the zoned orchis like a purple bee,

By the rich mountain-tulip's splendid wings

Dropt like a flame-tuft on the shelving crag :

By the grey headland o'er the crescent bay :

By the faint ripple of the island foam :

By the sails that swept so proudly up the
    sea,

By the stern galleys, pulsing golden oars,

By every tuneful wind and wasted wave,

By virgin innocence and vestal tears,

And by thine own immortal maidenhood :—

Ah, by remembrance of those asphodels—

The lily of the Elysian heroes' rest—

The asphodels flung groundward in dismay

From thy faint trembling hands and fingers
    pure,

What time the sudden chariot and wild
    steeds

Rolled as a whirlwind, rushing up behind,

While on thy bare and ivoried shoulder
    came

Their breathing like the bellows of a forge—

24

And he, the demon lover, from the car
Stept as a cloud of gloom, and in his folds
Wrapt thee, and night closed on thy radiant
    eyes.

O, I adjure thee by that day's despair,
By those torn flowers thy lonely mother
    found
In search for thee, scorched by the burning
    wheels:
Ah, fallen flowers, have pity on them and
    me!
Bethink thee, Queen, how on that day one
    rose
Fell, of all blooms that fell the sweetest
    bud,
The mystic rose of girlhood ne'er rebloomed,
Its virgin curtain broken, its dewdrops
    gone—
Ah, not of Orcus all the sceptred gloom,
The purple and the queendom and the gold,
Shall do away touch of those gracious days,

By the hum of Ætna, vineyard-clustered
    Ætna,
Flushing its grapes with subterranean fire,
Girdled with gleaming cities round its sides,
And the hewn houses of great marble gods,
By the Sicilian ocean, cold and clear,
Whose deeps outpass in azure Hellas' seas,
Whose nights have mellower moons and
    clearer stars,
Whose fountains gush from more enamelled
    meads,
Whereby the halcyon flits, a tissued gleam,
Bird of the rainbow : and the lovely land
Is as one great and golden orchard plain,
And haunted by some Genius, dropping
    balm,
Winged, as a nightjar wings o'er darkened
    moors
With plumes of silent flight.
                                    I make appeal
Beyond thy queendom and these nether
    shades :

Out past the gloomy grandeur of thy throne
I rise to other regions, other realms;
And my entreaty soars on eagle wing
Beyond the horizon barriers of the past.
I speak to one pale girl, who passed her hours
With wool and distaff at her mother's side
In the sweet long ago.   Still beats thy heart
The same behind the ruby-cinctured stole;
Although long years of judging guilty souls
Have given thy lips and brow a stony mask,
And changed thee in Medusa's loveliness
For Hebe's roseleaf dimples.   In those
     days
The dews of pity came in easy tears,
And slight occasion dimmed thy lucid eyes
And brimmed their fountains.   If athwart
     thy path,
Prone from the lofty nest, some callow bird
Lay shattered in unfeathered nakedness,
A sight for tears.   And tears thou couldst
     bestow,
If with the hunter's arrow in her flank,

27

With blood-drips, limping through the cork-
    woods came
A mild and sobbing fawn.   I half believe
That the shed glories of a wasted rose
Could make thee weeping-ripe for one dead
    flower.
Ah! what a change has come!   The wax
    grows steel.
But in thy stern heart pity is not dead,
But on her lies the dust of cruel years.
Be once again the girl compassionate,
And lay aside the inexorable queen,
To hear my prayer, if only for an hour.
While I unroll the tragedy of love
In bleeding accents set to burning chords,
In agonies which thrill along my string.
Oh, for the language of a god to prove
The enormous desolation I endure !
Had Phœbus half my pain, all hell would
    weep.
Or if I had the mighty Sun-god's touch,
Then would I sweep the lyre with such a stress

And storm of passion, such supreme despair,
Such wailing emphasis, that I would make
The woods, the waves, the lonely mountains
    weep,
And I would drown all Nature in remorse,
A Niobe of tears, that this should be.
Until the withered phantom, hungry Death,
Relenting latest of created things,
In utter pity sets his cage-door wide,
And lets my lark soar back to crystal heaven,
Regaining that clear region, where her nest,
Empty and orphan, waits Eurydice.

What scourge from heaven, what scorpion
    whip of hell
Out-venoms my bereavement? Surely none.
To lose her any way were giant woe:
To lose her thus, ineffable despair.
Torn from my lips upon her spousal morn,
In the climax of her utmost dearness slain:
Slain at love's loveliest moment, ere the cup
Of her sweet being had enriched my life.

The rites at Hymen's gate were barely done,
The incense smouldering yet, the wine
    undried,
And trickling ruddy from the altar face
In our libations.   Then the marriage train
Wound through the temple doors with
    choral hymn.
She, like a meadow-rose in bridal robes,
Light-hearted trips along the pastoral hills,
Her maidens round her, roses near the rose.
Sweet as the blushing planet of the dawn,
She went with hurrying footsteps, light
    and free,
In silken bents knee-deep and tufted thyme,
Nor knew within the sedge an adder coiled,
Nor saw she pressing death.   But that ill
    worm,
Evolving fanged and fiercely from the herb,
Mailed round in sapphire bars and speckled
    scale,
Kissed once her rosy feet, and kissed no more :
But gave my darling sleep, measureless sleep ;

And we stood round, like nations changed
    to rock,
With some new Gorgon horror frozen numb. '
Then wild lament arose along the hills,
And dirges came where hymeneals rang.
Lord of his kingdom, Love sang pæan then ;
Reft of his empire, we sing dirges now.
And, sobbing cadence of funereal gloom,
We wind her in the raiment of the dead,
The shrouded mantle of eternal sleep,
Ay me, the dear one.   Then as twilight
    fell,
With torch and taper rounded, crowned with
    yew,
Wailing we bore her to the cypress lines,
Sown with the urns and ash of fiery hearts
Of old-world lovers, cold and gone to
    dust.
Thither we bore her pallid on her bier,
A silver moon cradled in ebon cloud ;
And over her we sprinkled marigolds,
Flowers of the dead, stars on the sable pall ;

And there was one more gravestone, one
    more heart
Broken, and in the world no other change.

What right have I to live, so crushed with woe?
I dare not see the light now she is gone.
I hate to watch the flower set up its face.
I loathe the trembling shimmer of the sea,
Its heaving roods of intertangled weed
And orange sea-wrack with its necklace fruit ;
The stale, insipid cadence of the dawn,
The ringdove, tedious harper on five tones,
The eternal havoc of the sodden leaves,
Rotting the floors of Autumn.   I am weary,
Weary and incomplete and desolate.
To me Spring, sceptred with her daffodil,
Droops with a blight of dim mortality,
And the birds sing Death and Eurydice.

Ah, dear and unforgotten ! on the wind
Her voice comes often, low and sweet it
    comes,

In such a sigh as draws the yearning soul
Out of my breast to follow and float away,
To lean upon the storm with falcon wing,
To overtake the laggard moaning blast,
And clasp her in the whirlwind, shade to
    shade,
And ghost to ghost.   Then let us interlock
Our spectral limbs, and so in mutual flight
Rush at the sun and burn remembrance out.
Be thou effectual Lethe to our pangs,
O mighty fountain of primeval fire;
Father of lesser lights, compassionate,
Burn out, abolish our two weary souls!
Thou rollest on to rest the toiling stars.
The meteor of the morning doth untie
Her shining sandals on thy temple floor,
And fiery flakes fall from her golden locks.

Forsaken Orpheus, smite once more the lyre:
Sweep all thy echoing chords and make an
    end.
Let sorrow quell the deep and vanquish Fate.

Let song and pity, winged with burning
    words,
Prevail upon a storm of melody,
Melting the Queen's inexorable heart,
As wax before the furnace of my pain.

O thou, most regal, arch and arbitress
Of doleful nations, with thy mural crown,
Rod of dominion, orb of adamant,
Robed in the ruddy stain of vintage lees,
With garments like the morning fiery red—
I do adjure thee, lovely Proserpine,
Terrible Proserpine, and yet most lovely,
Release the viper-slain Eurydice,
Untimely taken and supremely loved:
Give her again to taste the gentle air,
Let me extort her from this rugged Hell.

Lo, on my brow the toil-drops start as rain,
Raised by the wrestling fervour of my prayer;
And all my blood beats in an agony
Of hope and expectation.   Ah! relent.

34

I see sweet pity dawning in thine eyes
Immortal.   O my Queen, on thee returns
Breath of the ancient meads, thy mother's
    smile,
The old, old days, the sweet, sweet times of
    eld.
Thou shalt relent.   O lady, is it much
To thin the frequence of thy crowded
    realms
By losing one poor captive, dearly loved ?
She will return after a few brief years
To thine eternity.   'Tis but one crumb
Pinched from the side of thy great loaf of
    death,
Daughter of Ceres ; but one grain of corn,
Which in this nether world all winter slept
To rise on wings of spring in glorious
    birth !

Clash, O my lyre, clash all thy golden chords!
For we have won !   I see the ghosts divide
To right and left a mighty lane of darkness

As from the utmost coasts of Acheron
Eurydice comes sailing like a star.
Dove of the cypress, come: my hungry
    soul
Awaits thee trembling with expanded arms.

THE MARCH OF GLORY

I HEAR the nations march,
  As sweeping autumn rain,
By laurel-garnished arch,
  And trophies of the slain.
To music proud and high,
      By Glory led,
The stern-eyed ranks go by,
  To her battle-fields of dead.
Her heroes and her soldiers rush to die
Madly upon the spears with martial ecstasy.

The clash of battle's psalm
  Dilates their veins to glow ;
As tempest rocks the calm
  Grey surge to fleece of snow.
With iron in each palm,
  Invincible they go.

37

I hear the nations march.
 Their ample ensign's fold,
Spread as an eagle's wing,
 Flaps out in heavy gold:
O'er sheeted targe and shield
 The banners gaily swing:
On to their latest field
 The advancing bugles ring.

Moving to victory with solemn voice,
With timbrels, and with drum-beat, and the
 noise
 Of myriads : each man listens
For the laughter of her joys,
  To each man glistens
  The glitter of her eyes,
The phantom Glory leads the proud array,
  They follow, as she flies,
  And without reck or fears
  Right on the vale of tears
   Go marching gay.

Love's music mingles with the martial hymn,
And all the pealing clarions breathe of him,
The mighty voice, that recks not time or
    years,—
Love that no Death can dim,
    Love that Death makes complete,
      Whose glory is immense,
    Whose laughter is passing sweet,
      Beyond the reach of sense.

The laughter of one, who kisses well. The
    laugh
Of a great king, who mows his foes as chaff,
The laugh of the feaster, who sings in his
    pleasure.
The laugh of the miser, arm-deep in his
    treasure.
The laugh of the lark, when the young beam
    breaks
      Its cloudy cover.
The laugh of the dreaming girl, who wakes
      And finds her lover.

39

Joy and Love and Triumph in their marching
    Thou shalt hear, as sounds
Of tempest thro' the giant pinewood searching,
    When the great clarion of the gale resounds.
March on with throbbing drums and bugle
       sigh,
    Let the flute peal, the royal trumpet swell;
Hail! we salute thee, Queen, about to die:
    Hail, Glory, and farewell!

A HYMN TO APHRODITE

Uranian Aphrodite, fair
　　From ripples of the ocean spray:
Sweet as the sea-blooms in thy hair,
　　Rosed with the blush of early day,
O hear us from thy temple steep,
Where Eryx crowns the Dorian deep.

Unfold the rapture of thy face,
　　No more thy lustrous eyes conceal:
But from the rivers of thy grace
　　The rich abundant joys reveal
Give us the treasures of thy rest,
Take us as children to thy breast.

41

Desired of all the ages long,
  As Morning young, as old as Fate
The kneeling world with choral song
  Has crowded round thy altar gate.
Thine are the seasons past and dumb,
And thine the unborn years to come.

We are not worthy to endure
  The fervour of thy burning eyes,
Thy perfect lips, thy bosom pure,
  Thy radiant aspect, sweetly wise.
Breathe balm upon our span of breath,
For thou art almost queen of death.

To thee, enwreathed with passion flowers,
  Our unreluctant prayers are given :
Thou art so near, when other powers
  Seem worlds away in frigid heaven :
They know not, for they live apart,
The craving tumult of the heart.

42

Thy altar needs no victim slain :
  It reeks not with the bleeding steer ;
Thy kingdom is no realm of pain,
  Thy worship is no creature's fear.
Yet art thou trebly more divine,
Needing no hecatombs of kine.

The empires wane, the empires grow :
  They prosper or they are dismayed :
Time lays their wrangling voices low,
  The victors and the vanquished fade.
The foam-wreath on the crested spray
Lasts but an instant less than they.

But thou abidest, in thy might
  Eternal, and a rainbow beam
Is round thy head ; and clusters bright
  Of orbs among thy tresses gleam :
Clothed in the garment of the sun,
Sweet as the star of day begun.

Parent of Nature, lovely queen,
　Awake the frozen land's repose,
Until the perfumed buds are seen
　With promise of the myriad rose.
Descend, and on thy halcyon wing
Unlock the fountains of the spring.

AMARANTH

WHEN I have done with hornet grief,
   Nor fear the blind-worm, envy's sting,
When graveward Lethe brings relief,
   And calms the love-god's fretful wing.

When I am clear of human kind,
   And slumber with the patient dead,
Will she, the cruel, care to find
   Where they have laid my lonely head?

And, once or twice, when spring is here,
   Forego some trivial social tie,
To bring my grave a niggard tear,
   The sequel of a scanty sigh?

45

Weep! just enough to give your eyes
　　A brightness, as of April rain :
One tear for all my thousand sighs,
　　And countless kisses given in vain.

Assign my solemn resting-place
　　Six moments of thy bustling day,
Between the drive, the mart, the race,
　　The rout, the concert, and the play.

Let worldlings and their world forget
　　To rule thee, darling, for an hour ;
Give me a fragment of regret,
　　Bring me some silly wayside flower.

And ask thy heart, that heart of steel,
　　How comes this man to sleep below ?
What phase of death was his to feel,
　　What shock of doom, what lethal blow ?

46

Speak in soft accents of thy friend ;
   Dear heart, he cannot vex thee now,
For lovers' quarrels surely end,
   When dust is on the lover's brow.

And let thy voice, I found so sweet,
   Discuss my fate, appraise my deeds ;
And garner in thy heart my wheat,
   And clean forget my idle weeds.

So let me feign and cheat my mind,
   That thou wilt so rehearse my tale,
That I may fancy thou art kind,
   When kindness is of small avail.

Say this—'I read, my ancient love,
   The record of thy name and years,
Graved on the slab thy rest above :
   'Tis brief—as brief as woman's tears.'

Say then—' The long and sweet desire,
   The fearless Hope, the granite Trust,
The poet's lips, the lover's fire,
   Are ended—in a little dust.

' My old dead love was good and kind,
   But he was broken down with woes :
And doubts upon his deeper mind
   Made havoc in my dreams of rose.

' I said, Ye ages, bring me then
   A perfect lover, rich and great,
A captain and a king of men,
   Unroll him, misty clouds of Fate.

' But this poor love of homespun gray,
   This honest heart, these faded eyes,
Come anywhen and any day—
   My beauty claims a lordlier prize.'

'He trod the humbler fields of time :
  How should he gain me gear or gold ?
How should this dullard hope to climb,
  Who hardly knew how Faith is sold ?

'He was no senate quack, who came
  To nibble at the public purse,
And rise, a charlatan, to fame
  By leaving bad a little worse.

'The balm of popular success
  Ignored his inconspicuous head,
The unction of the daily press
  In inky blessings ne'er was shed.

'He spun no cotton, owned no banks,
  He ran no racers, gave no balls,
He had no deer with dappled flanks
  To trot around his stuccoed halls.

' He came no king of beer to crowd
  The jostling streets with barrelled drays.
No huckster, full of promise, loud
  To sing the mighty Mammon's praise.

' Too proud to tell the rabble votes,
  That all the mob demands is true :
Too dull to learn the parrot notes
  Of Freedom from the last Review.

' Too slow to feign a patriot fire,
  Then clutch the prizes of the game ;
Or follow ankle-deep in mire
  The beckoning smile of spurious Fame.

' He did not trust some cherub black,
  To ope the *El Dorado* gate,
Nor went with every lantern jack,
  Who flickers o'er a festering State.

' He stood aside and watched the strife,
   Weary, and longing to depart :
He left, as assets of his life,
   The record of a wasted heart.

' At least he loved me : this concede :
   But I entrenched my soul in pride.
So when I scorned and would not heed,
   He drew Life's curtain down and died.

' Yet thro' the pleading of his vows
   Ambition whispered, " Do not yield,
He is as poor as some church mouse,
   I lead you to a golden field."

' Of all my lovers that remain,
   None loved me with so firm a zeal.
My shallow fancy could not feign
   A passion, which I dared not feel.

' He was too humble in his suit,
  And I too proud in my disdain ;
And now, because his lips are mute,
  I fain would hear their love again.

' I fain would have thee at my side,
  When Spring is reaching out her hands,
When April, like a weeping bride,
  Sails o'er the rosy orchard lands.

' When May winds bathe the reedy isles,
  Where swans are nesting with their broods,
And sheets of sapphire pave for miles
  The floors of hyacinthine woods.

' When sweet field-roses fringe the lane,
  And balmy hangs the incense thorn :
And, dreaming of ambrosial rain,
  The violet wakens, morn by morn,

52

' He will not wake, tho' snowdrops rise,
   Nor greet the woodland bells of blue :—
I hail thee, love, with streaming eyes,
   Adieu, my love ! my love, adieu !

' Thou canst not breathe the morning breath,
   Nor hear the bees about the bloom,
Nor see them settle on this wreath,
   My trembling fingers bring thy tomb.

' I bring thee amaranth and rue.
   I leave my garland and depart,
More bitter than the branch of yew
   The anguish of my aching heart.'

CIRCE

THIS is the fair witch Circe, queen divine,
The daughter of the Sun : her charming
    wand
Rests on her ivory shoulder at command :
She holds a chalice of enchanted wine,
The sweet wine sweeter from the rosy hand.
She sits within a grove of gray wych-elms,
And sings across the waves with siren breath,
To call her lovers in from twilight realms,
To crowd their foolish sails for love and death.
And near the rocking breakers, drear and
    dread,
She hath a lordly palace of delight,
And a rich chamber where her couch is spread
With gems like orient sunrise, flashing light ;

Ruby and opal, sard and sardonyx
In soft effulgence mix;
Beryl and chrysolite
Beam on her brow by night:
Her drowsy lips are kissed
By rays of amethyst.

A loom is in her chamber, purple-flecked
A giant web expands, whereon is wrought
Nature in all her colours, fancy-caught;
Above that web two Cupids rosy-necked,
Almost alive in tinted Parian rock,
Mingle their locks together, each gauzed wing
Trembles and fans with light aërial shock.
As when two bees within one peony swing,
These brother Loves embrace,
Rosed with the shadow of the rose's face.
With fragrant mouths they seem to inter-
    breathe,
And there is passion in their lips of stone,
That gives the icy marble living grace,
And flushes underneath:

As on the snow-cloud grows
The dawn's red undertone,
When lisping zephyr blows.

And on each image from a flickering fire
Of cedar logs and bay-wood heaped behind
Reddens the flame and shimmers at its spire.
But of those Loves is neither sculptured blind.
One holds a rose—that means long love
    desire :
One holds an asphodel—that means reward.
And on their brows is coral-berried yew,
An emblem harsh and hard,
That means—ah, well a day,—
For lovers false and lovers true,
Sleep and its cloudy pinions, silvering
The folded hands and sharpened faces gray,
Sleep on her raven wing :
Sleep that no magic flower can charm away,
Or make us rise again,
The ruined sons of Care :
The slain of Love, the slain

Of the huge hooks and arrows of Despair.
O asphodel, Elysian asphodel,
Bedding Adonis in his wounded pain,
Flower of the heroes' dell,—
Dead lovers these of thine,
My Circe fine,
They are beyond thy sway
Into a deeper day
Past, unremembered wrecks of vain desire,
And broken lutes of passion's golden lyre.
Thy might is ended where the grave begins,
And thy innocuous spells
Fall by the margin of the sea of sins,
Done with as empty shells.

Dead, ay, and done with, not thy beauty's
    beam
Can make these men arise :
Their feet are tangled in the nets of dream,
They cross the stream of sighs.
Canst thou put breath between those wasted
    lips

That hold the boatman's toll,
The ferry-coin, where uncouth Charon ships
The Lethe-sailing soul?
They end and thou abidest: in a shroud
They pass to dust.   New victims find thee
    fair:
Into thy net new shoals of tunnies crowd,
New moths fall burning from thy radiant hair.
These creatures of a day acclaim thee queen,
And for their span of time exalt thy power;
All nature lies before thee, fresh and green,
My locust to devour.
Siren of blood and tears, the road to thee
Is paved with bramble hooks that rend the
    feet,
Thy crystal breast is paradise to see,
Beyond all breath of roses thou art sweet.
Thy brows, more lovely than the rainbow, are
Woven with many a star
Of the delicious deadly asphodel,
That in thy tresses braided shines afar,
When thou dost weave thy spell:

Stern as Medea in her dragon car,
Or as Canidia fell :
Or cruel as Medusa's sculptured face,
Set on a targe of war.
But other days thou wearest childish grace
By contrast to ensnare,
Aping the startled fawn, whom bugles scare,
Blown in the dewy glade.
Or in some new disguise,
To allure deluded eyes,
Thou art the shrinking violet, half afraid,
That, in rathe April born,
Where icy winds complain,
Hardly unfolds her petals to the morn
Between the rainbow and the weep of rain.

What blind one, wearing eyes and wanting
    brain,
Wilt thou, pale Circe, conquer with thy
    spell ?
To whom are kisses given,
Until he holds thee beautiful as heaven,

Golden as gold, too sweet for words to
    tell.
And all his soul is in thy roseleaf hands,
Where thou a queen dost sit in soft repose,
Watching the radiant lands.
Thy shrine of Love is there
A charnel masked with rose,
Love guards the entrance fair,
Ringed round with rainbow glows.
'Tis Love disguised as Death
Sits masked in iris ray,
And under his rose wreath
The scanty locks grow gray.
His eyes are hollow dim,
As a glow-worm on a grave,
He is great, O kneel to him :
Great to slay, and great to save.
Beneath the altar floors
The poisoned adder waits.
Behind the agate doors,
And round the burnished gates
The mighty pythons coil.

And toads unsanctified
The precinct pavement soil,
And in the garlands hide.
The altar burns ; in rubied cup divine,
From perfumed chalice shed,
Pour out the glow of .thy enchanted wine,
Wine for the lovers, who have loved thee
     dear,
And come to wed :
A cup of consolation, deep and clear,
They need no second tasting : they are dead.

In saffron-coloured pride
For Hymen art thou clad,
My Circe, sweeter bride
Ne'er made a bridegroom glad.
Or draped in Fortune's robe,
Ruler of blood and breath,
Thy wheel directs the globe,
O Fortune, which art Death !
Thy paradise embowers
Faint Acherusian flowers,

The warlock's charms of might,
Dwale, henbane, aconite
From gardens of despair,
To be as orange blossom in thy hair,
Sweet deadly rose ;
Altar of Love wrapt round with hemlock
    band,
To whom exultant goes
Thy victim and thy bridegroom : to whose
    hand
Death shall divide his posies, as the bride
Divides her kisses bland,
In maiden pride.
Death shall assign the coral apples small,
The blooms of violet hue
And central orange anther, whence bees fall
Drowsy with poisoned dew,
This is the nightshade, and its night is drear.
It apes the honest ivy in its leaves,
And in its grapelets mocks the clusters clear,
That shade the brow of Bacchus ; when he
    weaves

Some drowsy nymph in tendril curls of vine;
What better bloom divine
Could drape our Circe for her couch attired,
And veil her gentle breast,
An Ariadne of all men desired,
But only god-caressed :
As she lies sparkling in her nuptial glory :
What tho' its leaves behind
With fang-froth yet be hoary,
Are not all lovers blind ?
'Tis but the cuckoo's kiss,
Which bathes the clematis,
Or the ragged robin often,
When east winds begin to soften.

And who art thou, enchantress, serpent fell,
Lamia, whose dazzling eyes
Draw as with cords the nations to thy spell
To perish ? Thou, who slayest with love-sighs
Thy foolish lovers : fast as summer flies
Drop in a cup of mead or hydromel,
Or tangle in the web Arachne ties.

O loveless vengeance, masked in Love's attire,

O hate, that stealest Passion's sweetest lyre.

Vampire, whose beauty ripens on much
    death,

Siren, whose throne is built with bones be-
    neath ;

Blaspheming, soiling, and degrading him

The ineffable, the crown, the ray

Of all things ; in whose absence heaven is
    dim,

Love, at whose effluence utmost earth is gay,

And the gray fountains flow,

And the rathe lilies blow ;

Love lays his emerald mantle on the hills,

Love pours his rich blood in the mountain
    rills :

He bathes in sunset colours the flushed sea,

Mighty and lord is he.

What dire Plutonian birth

On this bewildered earth

Gave breath and empire, baleful queen, to
    thee ?

Wild pæan shook the Eblis halls of fire,
When thou wert born: old woes,
Shadows and phantoms of outwept desire,
Long dead, from charnels rose.
Love on thy cradle smiled, a babe divine,
And watched thy infant breath,
Love bitter as Despair and sweet as wine.
Love bitter-sweet as Death.
Time guided thee a daughter of delight
Upon thy beaming way:
And hung thy hair with jewels, as the night
Is spangled with star-ray.
Time made thee lovelier than all paradise,
A drop of god's own dew,
Distilled into a rainbow from blue ice,
Where falcon never flew.
The vital pomp of may-time and of morn
Shall glitter in her eyes.
Princes shall sell their honour for her scorn,
And wreck their realms with sighs.
If she lament, the languid lilies stain,
If she deplore, rust gathers on the rose.

If she bewail, in sympathetic pain
Night weeping rings with philomela's
    woes.
The stars attend her dreams
And bathe her with repose,
She lies in silver beams
A flushed unopened rose.

HELLAS AND ROME

Of Greece the Muse of Glory sings,
   Of Greece in furious onset brave ;
Whose mighty fleets, on falcon wings,
   To vengeance sweep across the wave.

There on the mounded flats of Troy
   The hero captains of the morn
Come forth and conquer, tho' the boy
   Of Thetis keeps his tent in scorn.

There in the sweet Ionian prime
   The much-enduring sailor goes,
And from the thorny paths of time
   He plucks adventure like a rose.

67

There sits Atrides, grave and great,
  Grim king of blood and lust-deed done,
Caught in the iron wheels of Fate
  To hand the curse from sire to son.

A fated race!   And who are these
  With viper locks and scorpion rods,
Dim shades of· ruin and disease,
  Who float around his household Gods?

Alas, for wife and children small:
  Blood comes, as from the rosebush bloom;
The very dogs about his hall
  Are conscious of their master's doom.

Or see the fleet victorious steed
  In Pindar's whirlwind sweep along,
To whom a more than mortal meed
  Remains, the bard's eternal song.

What are the statues Phidias cast,
  But dust between the palms of Fate?
A thousand winters cannot blast
  Their leaf; if Pindar celebrate

Great Hiero, Lord of Syracuse,
  Or Theron, chief of Acragas,
These despots wisely may refuse
  Record in unenduring brass.

For Pindar sang the sinewy frame,
  The nimble athlete's supple grip;
He gave the gallant horse to fame,
  Who passed the goal without a whip,

The coursers of the island kings
  Jove-born, magnanimously calm:
When gathered Greece at Elis rings
  In pæan of the victor's palm.

69

Or hear the shepherd bard divine
 Transfuse the music of his lay
With echoes from the mountain pine,
 And wave-wash from the answering bay.

And all around in pasturing flocks
 His goatherds flute with plaintive reeds,
His lovers whisper from the rocks,
 His halcyons flit o'er flowery meads:

Where galingale with iris blends
 In plumy fringe of lady fern;
And sweet the Dorian wave descends
 From topmost Ætna's snow-bright urn.

Or gentle Arethusa lies,
 Beside her brimming fountain sweet,
With lovely brow and languid eyes,
 And river lilies at her feet.

Or listen to the lordly hymn,
    The weird Adonis, pealing new,
Full of the crimson twilight dim,
    Bathed in Astarte's fiery dew.

In splendid shrine without a breath
    The wounded lovely hunter lies :
And who has decked the couch of death ?
    The sister-spouse of Ptolemies.

We seem to hear a god's lament,
    The sobbing pathos of despair :
We seem to see her garments rent,
    And ashes in ambrosial hair.

Clouds gather, where the mystic Nile,
    Seven-headed, stains the ambient deep.
The chidden sun forgets to smile,
    Where lilies on lake Moeris sleep.

Slumber and Silence cloud the face
  Of Isis in gold-ivory shrine :
And Silence seems to reach the race,
  Whose youth was more than half divine.

'Tis gone—The chords no longer glow :
  The Bards of Greece forget to sing ;
Their hands are numb, their hearts are slow :
  Their numbers creep without a wing.

Their ebbing Helicons refuse
  The droplet of a droughty tide.
The fleeting footsteps of the Muse
  We follow to the Tiber side.

The Dorian Muse with Cypris ends :
  With Cypris wakes the Latian lyre :
And, sternly sweet, Lucretius blends
  Her praise inspired with epic fire.

72

To thee, my Memmius, amply swells
   Rich prelude to her genial power,
Her world-renewing force, which dwells
   In man, herd, insect, fish, or flower.

Supremely fair, serenely sweet,
   The wondering waves beheld her birth,
The power, whose regal pulses beat
   Thro' every fibre of the earth.

Why should we tax the gods with woe,
   They sit outside, they bear no part?
They never wove the rainbow's glow,
   They never built the human heart.

These careless idlers who can blame?
   If Chance and Nature govern men:
The universe from atoms came,
   And back to atoms rolls again.

73

As earthly kings they keep their state,
   The cup of joy is in their hands;
The war-note deepens at their gate,
   They hear a wail of hungry lands.

They feast, they let the turmoil drive,
   And Nature scorns their fleeting sway:
She ruled before they were alive,
   She rules when they are passed away.

Before the poet's wistful face
   The flaming walls of ether glow:
He sees the lurid brinks of Space,
   Nor trembles at the gulfs below.

He feels himself a foundering bark,
   Tossed on the tides of Time alone.
Blindly he rushes on the dark,
   Nor waits his summons to be gone.

74

Wake, mighty Virgil, nor refuse
  Some glimpses of thy laurelled face :
Sound westward, wise Ausonian Muse,
  The epic of a martial race.

Grim warriors, whom the wolf-dug rears,
  Strong legions, patient, steadfast, brave,.
Who meet the shock of hostile spears,
  As sea-walls meet the trivial wave.

Justice and Peace their highest good,
  By sacred law they held their sway,
The ruler's instinct in their blood
  Taught them to govern and obey.

They crushed the proud, the weak they spared,
  They loosed the prostrate captive's chain :
And civic rights and birthright shared
  Made him respect their equal reign.

75

They grappled in their nervous hands
  The nations as a lump of dough :
To Calpe came their gleaming bands,
  To Ister grinding reefs of snow.

And where the reedy Mincius rolled
  By Manto's marsh the crystal swan,
There Maro smote his harp of gold,
  And on the chords fierce glory shone.

The crested metre clomb and fell ;
  The sounding word, the burnished phrase
Rocked on like ocean's tidal swell,
  With sunbeam on the water-ways.

He sang the armoured man of fate,
  The father of eternal Rome,
The great begetter of the great,
  Who piled the empire yet to come.

He sang of Daphnis, rapt to heaven,
　At threshold of Olympian doors,
Who sees below the cloud rack driven,
　And wonders at the gleaming floors.

He sang the babe, whose wondrous birth,
　By Cumæ's sibyl long foretold,
Should rule a renovated earth,
　An empire and an age of gold.

He sang great Gallus, wrapt in woe,
　When sweet Lycoris dared depart
To follow in the Rhineland snow
　The soldier of her fickle heart.

The nectared lips that sang are mute,
　And dust the pale Virgilian brows,
And dust the wonder of the lute,
　And dust around the charnel-house.

77

Above the aloes spiring tall,
　　Among the oleander's bloom,
Urned in a craggy mountain hall,
　　The peasant points to Virgil's tomb.

The empire, which oppressed the world,
　　Has vanished like a bead of foam ;
And down the rugged Goths have hurled
　　The slender roseleaf sons of Rome.

For ages in some northern cave
　　The plaintive Muse of herdsmen slept,
Till, waking by the Cam's wise wave,
　　Once more her Lycid lost she wept.

As pilgrims to thy realm of death,
　　Great Maro, we are humbly come,
To breathe one hour thy native breath,
　　To scan the lordly wreck of Rome.

And, tho' thy Muses all are fled
    To some uncouth Teutonic town,
Sleep, minstrel of the mighty dead,
    Sleep in the fields of thy renown.

A WINTER SKETCH

WHEN the snow begins to feather,
  And the woods begin to roar,
Clashing angry boughs together,
  As the breakers grind the shore.
Nature then a bankrupt goes,
Full of wreck and full of woes.

When the swan for warmer forelands
  Leaves the sea-firth's icebound edge :
When the gray geese from the moorlands
  Cleave the cloud in noisy wedge.
Woodlands stand in frozen chains,
Hung with ropes of solid rains.

Shepherds creep to byre and haven,
　　Sheep in drifts are nipped and numb :
Some belated rook or raven
　　Rocks upon a sign-post dumb.
Mere-waves solid as a clod
Roar with skaters thunder-shod.

All the roofs and chimneys rumble,
　　Roads are ridged with slush and sleet ;
Down the orchard apples tumble,
　　Ploughboys stamp their frosty feet.
Millers, jolted down the lanes,
Hardly feel for cold their reins.

Snipes are calling from the trenches,
　　Frozen half and half at flow,
In the porches servant wenches
　　Work with shovels at the snow.
Rusty blackbirds, weak of wing,
Clean forget they once could sing.

Dogs and boys fetch down the cattle,
　　Deep in mire and powdered pale:
Spinning wheels commence to rattle,
　　Landlords spice the smoking ale.
Hail, white winter, lady fine,
In a cup of elder wine.

A SONG OF DUST

WHEN we, my love, are gone to dust,
   And nature, as of old, is fair :
When on thy rosy cheek is rust,
   And stain sepulchral on thy hair.

When from the slab, that marks our sleep,
   The raindrop eats our names away :
And cushioned lichens gently creep
   To make the beaming letters gray.

When March winds wake the silken palm,
   And wave-worn wheatears skim the sea.
When merles begin their marriage psalm,
   And doves are tender in the tree.

When, year by year, the mosses bloom
   Their little elfin caps of red :
And April dewdrops on thy tomb
   Weep out in daisies o'er the dead ;

These tears, I weep upon thy hand,
   Shall pass as leaves in autumn air.
And who unborn shall understand,
   If thou wert sweet, if thou wert fair ?

Who shall embalm thee in a song
   A hundred years to cheat repose ?
Oblivion rolls its flood along,
   Till Time forgets one wasted rose.

Who shall explain this lovely thing
   To generations yet to be ?
Will evanescent beauty wing
   Her flight to dim futurity ?

No lease is hers of lengthened hours :
  Her love a momentary ray,
Crisping the calyx of the flowers,
  Is sped before the lift of day.

A little while the whitethorn blows,
  And all the grasses rarely spring.
Then crimsons out the wild field rose,
  And swallows rest their travelled wing.

And fair are maidens in their prime ;
  And lovers pledge eternal truth,
When for an hour the cup of Time
  Is nectar on the lips of youth.

Love and the nest of birds are sweet ;
  Till, like a broken hope, the flower,
Warm at the early sunbeam's feet,
  Lies shattered cold at evening's hour.

No perfect joy thy life endears.
    What light is thine? Some casual gleam,
Which, rising thro' a mist of tears,
    Falls on the phantoms of thy dream.

All shall forget thee, as a breath
    From clover meadows richly shed;
Divine as coloured evening's death,
    Thy cheek will lose its lustrous red.

Pale as a wreath of alpine snows,
    She lies in marble silence sweet,
When rigid Death doth interpose
    The stark and long-drawn winding sheet.

O region of the moonless grave,
    Lonely and lurid is thy home,
Where Love, who came so fresh and brave,
    Is narrowed in with shelving loam.

Love old and gray and nearly blind
　　Among the mounds, whose bleeding feet
The fangs of winding brambles bind,
　　The hooks of bitter roses meet.

And Pride, with all her trophies torn,
　　Hangs o'er a funeral urn to weep
The devious night, the tardy morn,
　　Belated in the paths of sleep.

And eyes, that dim the violet made,
　　Forget to shed their gracious rays:
When, on each darkened eyelid's shade,
　　The midnight of oblivion weighs.

The ages in an endless tide
　　Advance their still encroaching feet:
The present, like a golden bride,
　　Is faultless for an hour and sweet.

87

Time will not stay for thee, my love,
  The clouds are coming and the snow ;
The thunder rocks the realms above—
  One farewell kiss before we go.

     .   .   .   .   .   .

A song of dust for waning years,
  A solemn song in sackcloth clad :
Whose chords are wet with poignant tears,
  And its pale singer's lips are sad.

THE DEATH OF PHAETHON

PHAETHON, HAVING PERSUADED . HIS FATHER, HELIOS, TO
ALLOW HIM TO DRIVE THE CHARIOT OF THE SUN FOR
ONE DAY, STARTS ON HIS JOURNEY.

BEFORE him the immeasurable heaven
Lay deep and boundless.   The eternal stars,
Pulsing and throbbing in the blue profound,
Grew nearer.   Slow revolving lights of
    heaven,
Their golden spheres with moony clusters
    mixed,
Made orbit; and, beyond, as amber dust,
A sprinkling of innumerable globes,
Sown on the outward limits of the void :
Beyond all computation and account,
The seed and drift of undeveloped worlds,
In their bright millions rolling on their way.

89

The wonder of that wilderness of god
Flushed all his face, as swiftly rolled the car.
So slides some fleecy cloud along the dawn,
When the young east grows rosy, and wild
    rain
Wrecks half the mountain woods and rends
    the pines.

So in his brief and baleful hour of joy,
The boy exulted in the soaring rush
Of that celestial road : he joyed to feel
The mighty long-haired coursers of the sun
At his command, and all their speed his own.
The gleaming chariot his: the pomp of
    heaven,
His : in his veins the ichor of a god
Seemed to dilate his pulse with spirit fire.
And with an easy rein his hand could guide
Time and Dominion: his to wake the
    world,
His to refresh the flushed auroral light
In splendid waves and cloud of purple foam,

A glorious task, well worth a god's control,
To wake the dewy fields and oceans old,
And lift the veil from Morning's violet eyes.

Then the rash boy in arrogant disdain
Shook the bright reins and shouted impious
    words
Behind the horses, nor the lash refrained ;
Vain-glorious, clouded with the madding
    fume
Of ill-accustomed honour. He would climb
God with the godlike now. Too long withheld
He grasped his birthright : all the bitter past,
Sordid, obscure, the delving, rustic days,
The dark dim days with herds and vacant
    boors,
End in the nectar cup and festal heaven.

As when the rathe and poignant spring divine
Sighs all too soon among the hoary woods,
And from the fleecy drifts of sodden snow
With promise and with perfume calls her buds,

And the buds open when they hear her feet,
And open but to perish.   So his heart
Bloomed in a burst of immortality,
Nor feared the onward rolling vans of doom.
Yearning he had and hunger to ascend,
To sit at endless feast, with purple robes
To fold his limbs in sheer magnificence.
With rays of glory round his radiant hair,
And deity effulgent in his brows :
A dream divine, whose passionate desire
Flooded his soul, till in the golden car
He trembled at the vision : as a leaf
Moved by a gale of splendour, that comes on,
When, at the point of sunrise, the wind
    sweeps
With sudden ray and music across the sea.
So in that rapture of presumptuous joy
He spake a dreadful and an impious word ;
That he was nature's lord and king of gods,
He cared not now for Zeus, how should he
    care ?
Let the old dotard nod and doze above.

He rode the morning in unchecked career,
Apparelled in his sire's regalities,
The new Hyperion, greater than his sire ;
While the swift hooves beat music to his
    dream :
And for a little while his heart was glad,
Throbbing Olympian ichors.   For an hour
Elate, he bore an ecstasy too great
For mortal nerve, and knew the pride of
    gods.

The rushing air came on his brows, the deep
Ether around him rustled in his ears.
Among those awful solitudes, on, on,
The headlong onset of his coursers swept.
Light and the speed drew dimness on his
    eyes :
And, in the flakes and sparkles of the wheels,
He drove as in a fountain drift of fire,
Orbed in a splendid shower of lambent gold ;
He bore it not for long, an icy chill
Crept upwards inch by inch against his heart,

And formless horror deepened up behind ;
Unguessed as yet, more awful from the
    shroud,
That hid its spectral features, creeping on.
Then impious exultation flared and fled,
And shuddering he beheld before his mind,
No nectar cup but Charon's charnel boat.
And the rose visions on his region clouds
Unpurpled all their gates, and gathered in
A core of thunder ripening ragged brows.
He saw and he despaired : an abject fear
Perplexed the demigod, who lately rode
Vaunting himself so proudly : now dismayed,
And horribly confounded in the toils
Of the great net his upstart pride had spread.

But when the horses guessed their driver's fear,
And felt the reins that shuddered in his
    grasp,
A grievous panic dimmed their dauntless
    mood,
In anger at the feeble charioteer.

Then with mad impulse and a headlong ire,
They scorned control, and swept resistless
    on——
Who shall assuage them now? Not Her-
    cules,
Not Atlas shoring up the beams of heaven.
And all the chariot rocked from side to side,
And he, who guided, quailed upon his bench;
For these ethereal coursers, panic-wild,
Felt not his check and heeded not his rein
More than the pressure of a lighted fly.
He might as well pull back some granite
    cliff,
Athos unroot, dislodge Pelorus huge :
Or drag some river python from his ooze,
As set his weakling hand to check or chain
The corded sinews of their iron necks.
How could he calm their nostrils, snorting
    out
The cloudy vapour of resentful ire ?
He found no balm, no comfort, no resource :
And so with ineffectual fingers numb,

Gave them reluctant way and let them sweep,
Through splendid zones of flushing roseate
    haze ;
He heeded not their splendour : he beheld
The glimmer of his last poor rushlight hope
Abolished, vanished, blotted out, extinct.
He saw the vengeance of the sire supreme
Reach in red anger at his armories,
To unlink the sleeping thunder. And he
    knew,
That from the gloomy oracles of Jove
Doom had gone out on his presumptuous
    head.

Then scorning curb at such a nerveless hand,
The mighty steeds, who bring the beam of
    morn,
In furious speed, revolting, broke away,
Straining the reins and loosening on the void
Flakes of dim foam, shed off like little clouds :
Wide-eyed, dishevelled, tossing their lithe
    heads,

And ruffling out the tangle of their manes,
Groaning and heaving, vapoured in a breath
Of effort, toiling as immortals tòil :
And down their panting flanks the heat-drops
    rolled.

Then those undaunted horses first knew fear,
And cloudy horror vexed their mighty hearts,
When they perceived, Fate, mother of sur-
    prise,
Had made the sacred process of the sun
The plaything of a fool to steer or wreck,
With novice hand : an earthborn charioteer,
Usurping the Titanic chariot-bench,
To shatter on the void immense abyss
The fragments of the sun's triumphal march.
What time the fool himself, this spurious god,
Rocking and swaying in the chariot floor,
Clutched at the golden rail with palsied hand.
As some clown drunk with fumes of trodden
    wine,
When the red vats unpurple all the hills,

And the must trickles down to pipe and song,
As the rude orgies of the wake begin.
So stood he dazed and heaved a painful
 breath,
That caught and laboured harshly in his
 throat.
Not less between his parched and livid lips
The torment of immeasurable thirst
Raged as a flame, and greatened as they flew.
While, matting his half-girlish forehead curls,
The dew of his distress lay beaded cold.

But far away beneath those burning wheels,
Came up a gentle whisper of sea waves,
Murmur and ripple of music dimly heard,
And pleasant shocks of foam : and shaken
 bells
On the faint pastoral hills by curving shores,
And dim gray forelands steeped in roseate
 haze :
And the white fisher cities, perched as birds,
In nooks and margins of the mighty seas

At rest : the reed-thatched homes of humble
    men,
Who never cloudward soared, but in content
Lived on the fickle favour of the waves ;
And ploughed for harvest in the heaving
    fields
Of rolling Neptune and his gray-green realms.

But neither restful peace nor human joy
Lived in the aspect of thy anguished eyes,
Sad son of Phœbus, on whose rash career
The inevitable silence crushing came
To numb thee round in huge Pythonian coils.
Then in one supreme effort for his life,
Fiercely he set his ebbing strength to stem
That awful chariot race, where Hades sat
As arbiter, adjudging wreaths of yew.
Yet vain his effort ; cut with leathern thongs,
He dropped his bleeding fingers, maimed and
    torn.
And those wild coursers swept remorseless on,
Because a fool had teased and angered them,

To end rebuke and the rebuker there,
And wreck themselves, and shed this ape of
    gods,
Prone upon ether like a flake of snow.

Then the sad wretch, seeing his hour was
    come,
Called on his father in a hoarse wild cry,
Between a sigh and sob, most dire to hear :
And from his aching hands, relaxed with
    toil,
He dropt the useless wrestle of the reins.
They, fluttering in a downward tangle, fell,
And caught among the traces and the hooves :
And snapt and cracked, and the fierce horses
    plunged,
Jumbled in wreck, and rolled with frantic
    feet.
Then came a crash, as when thro' sodden
    clouds,
Tearing and hissing the blue bol descends ;
And on some towering temple's long façade

Lights in red vengeance, hurling from the
    frieze
Its marble god, the genius of the fane ;
So with a deafening peal of thunder shock,
The dazzling Delian car was overturned,
Wondrous, eternal, treasure-house of rays,—
Which even gods revere and men adore
With suppliant knee, as in itself a god—
Wrecked, ruined, drifted on the idle winds,
No better than an infant's broken toy :
Into the cloud abyss that racked below,
Shed as a dew-bead on a spider's raft.
And, headlong from the splintered chariot-
    bench,
The charioteer fell like a fluttered leaf ;
Or as a feather shaken from the wing
Of some high-soaring eagle, when the hail
Falls in a whirlwind and the woods cry back.

So fell the doomed one, reaching to his sire
An ineffectual heap of yearning arms,
His father aidless at the pinch of need,

Remote and far away in idle heaven ;
Lapt in amaracus and asphodel,
Lotus and oleander and musk-rose :
Reclined at endless feast, and had no heed,
Purpling with nectar draughts his lip divine,
And thought not on his agonising son.

So helpless and so headlong didst thou fall,
Weak heart, unequal to the fiery helm,
A rush of heaving limb and fluttered robe,
Rolling and spinning like a plummet down
Into the spacious gulf of deep blue air :
Poor mortal fool, masked in a god's attire,
To die in borrowed trappings not thine own.
And as a diver, plunging down, divides
The columned wall of waters with his weight,
Which close in swift reunion, as he sinks,
Above his headlong passage to the pearl,—
Where the fell shark, that floating dragon,
    guards
The rich Hesperian orchards of the main—
So, through the cloudy stories of the sky,

Long purple belts and blood-red vapour lines,
Fell Phaethon ; as falls some Pleiad lost,
Dead from the dance her starry sisters weave:
And, falling, in his horror he beheld
Merciless crag and angry precipice,
Waiting to rend him. Underneath, the
    earth
Rushed up to meet him with incredible
    speed,
Till one green field like lightning came at
    him,
Struck his brow wildly and dashed him into
    dead,
Shapeless and shattered, void of glory now,
Red clay to-day, to-morrow a little dust.

Ay me, ay me, now let the wail begin.
Where is the bright young god, the lovely
    where ?
The sweet limbs like a maiden's, very white,
The cheek one rose-leaf ? The young voice
    like song ?

Crushed lies the hand that thought to guide
    the sun :
Still the proud heart and cold the marble
    lips,
Thirsting in vain the chalice of the
    gods.
Ay me, ay me ; so must it always end,
When man, the mock of doom, this fleeting
    shade,
Disdains the narrow pinfold of his fate :
And breaks his heart in vain attempts to
    scale
The rampart of the adamantine rocks,
Whereon the careless Zeus sits calm and
    crowned.
Low art thou fallen, hapless Phaethon ;
Be merciful, ye flowers, and cover him :
Be silent, birds and bees: gray fountains
    weep :
Let his fair sisters come with wild lament,
And in their fresh hands bring the cypress
    bough,

And let the dirge begin.   Thou shalt be
    mourned,
More than Idalia mourned her shepherd lost.
And softly on thy urn shall fall the tear
Of kindred maidens.   They shall wrap thy
    limbs
In costly cerements, as a monarch's son;
And hide thy ashes in a marble tomb,
And give thee yearly rites and garlands due;
As, in the train of each revolving spring,
This sad day lives again ; and men shall tell
Thy story thro' the never-ending years.

ANTHEA'S GARLAND

Roses, bright with tears of rain,
  Which Anthea's tresses bind,
Proudly in her service slain,
  Shed your blossoms on the wind.

Petals, pure as ocean shell,
  Leaf by leaf must fall away :
As from raptured philomel,
  Note by note, descends her lay,

Cadence shaken on the gale,
  Fragments of divine desire,
When the enamoured nightingale
  Breaks her heart against a brier.

So let my Anthea's wreath
   Perish with a royal doom,
Wasted by the May-god's breath,
   Dirged by zephyrs to its tomb.

Die and break upon her breast,
   Where the sister roses lie ;
Perish near the ambrosial nest,
   Where a dove might come to die.

Till she turn her lustrous eyes
   Downwards on each ruined flower,
Musing with a world of sighs—
   ' Love is broken in an hour.

' Let me sing thy requiem,
   Wasted wreath, which bound my hair,
Roses pleasant on the stem,
   Sweetened in the crystal air.

'Let me speak your epitaph,
  Garland roses, soon to die.
On the maiden's heedless laugh,
  Comes the mother's anxious sigh.

'Gay to-day and gray to-morrow,
  Sad at eve, at morning blithe,
Runs the burden of our sorrow,
  While the Time-God whets his scythe.

'Not in scorn or idle laughter
  Empty solace will I seek ;
As this faded wreath, hereafter
  Soon will fade my damask cheek.

'In Youth's iris-purpled spaces
  Lovers join their lips in trust :
In the realm of faded faces
  Youth and Love return to dust.

'Hail, ye soon dismembered roses,
  Hail, dishevelled wreath forlorn.
In the gracious garden closes
  Noon repairs the wrecks of morn.

'Soon they blow and soon they perish,
  Bud and bloom and melt as snows.
And this god, whom maidens cherish,
  Love, is briefer than a rose.'

So she mused and so she ended,
  First she laughed and then she frowned,
For the garland, once so splendid,
  Lay in fragments on the ground.

THE FIRST MADRIGAL

COME away, O gentle breast,
   Who can tell if Love will stay ?
As the purple in the west,
   Love at even fades away :
As the breaker's foam-wreath crest
   Cannot keep its iris ray.

Bloom at ease, most radiant rose,
   Spread thy splendour flushed with light ;
Will the cloudy verge disclose
   Halcyon skies for ever bright?
Who can tell, what drifted snows
   Menace from the deep-browed night?

Fear the fiercely driving rack
   With its drench of swollen hail ;
Who shall build thy petals back,
   If they fall beneath its flail,
Shattered, in a whirlwind's track,
   Ruined rosebud of the vale ?

Will the gnawing canker's hate
   Blight the buds, tho' tempest spare ?
Beauty has no certain date :
   If one instant she is fair,
Lapsing Time and wheeling Fate
   Change her grandeur to despair.

Love, who burning came at noon,
   Coldly turns at eve to go.
When the golden hours of June
   Change into the month of snow,
Weeping Love forgets too soon
   Kisses, which he used to know.

Pale his cheek, his eyes are 'dim,
　　Sick he lies and like to die.
Lute and harp, make dirge for him,
　　Where the yellowing wood-leaves lie :
Colder grows each noble limb ;
　　Call, he cannot now reply.

Calm he lies in marble sleep,
　　Shrouded round with branching yew :
His sad eyes in slumber deep,
　　Our sad eyes the tears bedew :
For the Love-Lord, weep, O weep,
　　Gather rosemary and rue.

AN ODE TO A STAR

SWEET weary pilgrim of the heavenly places,
　Star of the gray, pursuing rosy flight :
Roaming the vast secluded planet spaces
　Among the spheres of night :

Thou art all silver-zoned, and radiant-breasted,
　Veiled round with refluent hair :
Thy train is meteor dust, thy forehead
　　crested
　With blue-gold beacon glare.

As beams, which from a leaden storm-rift
　　curtain
　Silver the ocean gray :
As a ship-light, that wrestles in the uncertain
　Furrows of shifting spray—

H　　　　　　　113

Thou wendest on, and wilt not die, tho'
    vapour
  Eat at thy heart, and haze
Perplex thy dim refluctuant earnest taper,
  And shake its tortured rays.

Till for its toil it touch deep rest as payment,
  Queen of its devious way.
As some fair child, rose-cheeked, with
    brightened raiment,
  And fragrant-breathed as May.

Sweet shall it share then in its sisters' singing,
  As a star only sings:
Where, round some palace, like bright swal-
    lows clinging,
  Hang clustered angel wings:

Calm shall ungird its sandal-strings of going,
  Fold its worn plumes of flight,
And sleek its breast against the overflowing
  Frondage of primal light.

Thus is my song, a lone and wandering meteor,
  Roaming thro' cloud and breeze ;
As in a wild March morn the wave-worn wheatear
  Scents haven overseas.

Song of a star, as from some censer shaken,
  Thy perfumed incense blows,
And, rolled aloft, while lights auroral waken,
  Reflects their purple glows.

VENGEANCE

My lady came in mournful plight,
And told me, how some courtly knight
Had gabbled o'er her blameless name
The censure of a shameless shame.

And, as she told his hideous lies,
And rainy sorrow brimmed her eyes,
Upon my sword, beside her laid,
She wept three tears against the blade.

I raised the hilt, and, nothing loth,
Upon its cross I sware an oath :
My lips impressed the holy spot,
The oath, then sworn, was not forgot.

Next morn, the sacred tears reveal
Three rust-spots on the naked steel.
Now, there are other stains below,
They are the life-blood of her foe.

A SERENADE

PEACE, where my love reposes,
 A shrine of slumber gray ;
Let sleep repair her roses
 Torn by the stress of day.
Sleep, till orient skies
  Misty peaks discover,
  Calling back thy lover,
 Where afar he lies,
  Thy lonely lover.

When will my love awaken,
 And beam her light on me,
Like a mighty sunbeam shaken
 On a dark and shuddering sea ?

Drifts of fiery cloud
    Round the mountain smoulder
    Veils of sleep enfold her,
    Like a rosy shroud
      Around a rosy shoulder.

Peace be thine and blessing,
    A peace I cannot share,
In troubled dreams caressing
    A phantom maid of air.
Melt out, old night, and pass,
    And sow the mountain places
    With tufted primrose faces;
    Then bring the real lass
      To my embraces.

THE SECOND MADRIGAL

Woo thy lass while May is here,
　　Winter vows are colder.
Have thy kiss when lips are near,
　　To-morrow you are older.

Think, if clear the throstle sing,
　　A month his note will thicken :
A throat of gold in a golden spring
　　At the edge of the snow will sicken.

Take thy cup and take thy girl,
　　While they come for asking.
In thy heyday melt the pearl,
　　At the love-ray basking.

Ale is good for careless bards,
Wine for wayworn sinners.
They, who hold the strongest cards,
Rise from life as winners.

INFATUATION

To dote upon some silent star for years,
  Shrined in remotest galaxies above,
Will bring thee less remorse and fewer tears,
  Than her cold scorn, harsh echo to thy
    love.

Rush to embrace the rainbow still retreating,
  And at the fen-fire's flicker warm thy hand;
Till marble-heart shall bring thee pleasant
    greeting,
  Go twist the sea-dunes into ropes of sand.

Why dost thou love this lumpish block of
    stone?
  Why gauge the pulses in that shallow
    breast?
Why make thy fruitless suit, with such a
    moan,
  As turtles mourn their raven-plundered
    nest?

Ask pity sooner from the hail, the cloud;
  And bid the bitter wind spare sail and sea;
The clay-cold maid shall waken in her
    shroud,
  And bring her lips, ere thou bring thine,
    to me.

I may persuade the tiger from his hate,
  And make the viper gentler than the dove,
And train a wolf as watch-dog at my gate,
  Ere thy flint heart respond one note of
    love.

Make, if thou canst, the ravening vulture
    kind,
And call the kite to leave her carrion slain ;
'Twill waste thy pains and harass less thy
    mind,
Than sottish love and obdurate disdain.

THE TOMB: AN ALLEGORY

I saw a woman with an infant stand
   Outside the portal of a vaulted tomb,
   And on its door were written words of
     doom,
And a vast silence deepened o'er the land.
Then, turning to that child, she gave com-
     mand
   To kneel beside her at the gate of gloom,
   And lay before that charnel wreaths of
     bloom,
And press those doors of death with kisses
     bland.

' I am the life that gave him to the grave:
And this poor child, the pledge of our
    despair,
On whom a father's smile might never dwell—
Thou hero, whom immortals could not save,
Tho' Love was sweet and Time was very
    fair,
Thine be the lilies of the asphodel.'

ANTICIPATION

I SET my heart to sing of leaves,
  Ere buds had felt the March wind blow :
I laid my head and dreamt of sheaves,
  Ere seedsmen had the heart to sow :
I fancied swallows at the eaves,
  And found old nests in pendent snow.

I dreamt a scent of daffodils,
  When frosty shone the village tiles :
Of flowery perfume from the hills,
  When ice had bound the mere for miles :
Of kingcups yellowing all the rills,
  When snowdrift silted up the stiles.

127

I found a barren bush of thorn,
  Where hung last year the sweet field-rose:
I said, no hint of purple morn
  The chambers of the east disclose:
Poor heart, poor song, poor pinions torn,
  Flutter and perish in the snows.

I said, a winter, huge and deep,
  Crawls on the bitter, hungry plain:
Why should I dream, who cannot sleep,
  Or hope to understand the pain,
Which rolls the doleful tears I weep,
  That Spring is dead, that Love is slain?

A CHURCHYARD YEW

BRIGHT levels of the wandering wave
  Behind the russet sails,
  How soon your burnish fails :
Soon die the damask-amber glows,
Isled on a galaxy of rose,
  In splendid veils.

Sad yew-tree, sister of the grave,
  Black upas nursed on death,
  Thy root draws mandrake breath,
Thy windy branches creak, and tell
In what fat bitter soil they dwell,
  Who sleep beneath.

Thy feet grim sloping gravestones pave :
   Thy bole salt crystals smear
   With scurf of briny tear :
Thy gnarled and torture-twisted form
Shrinks landward from the scathing storm,
   Year after year.

But here are girls and soldiers brave
   Beneath the sods at calm :
   And lovers here, whose psalm
The dismal silence long hath dulled,
And here is Sorrow lapt and lulled
   In slumber's balm.

The robin whistles on a grave,
   His throat with song distended ;
   A butterfly has wended
To some *hic jacet*, where he clings
To close and open shuddering wings
   With borders splendid.

Thou heedest not the wild bird's stave,
  Old bitter broken tree,
  Thou feedest not the bee.
Thou drawest from thy soil of blight
A deadly apathy, and Night
  Environs thee.

Here, as the wild green breakers rave,
  Thy berry, fleshed in red,
  Hangs down its poisoned head ;
There squeaking bats in gloom carouse,
And, roosted in thy charnel boughs,
  The owl 's in bed.

The mole is working in her cave,
  By glowworm taper shine,
  She graveward drives her mine.
And, on a wreath of faded roses,
A lean old rat to these discloses
  How he shall dine.

Cold stars above their glimmer save :
  And haggard is the moon
  To hear the raven's tune—
How soon must Love and Glory rust,
And rosy lasses come to dust
  And slumber soon.

THE HAUGHTY LADY CONDEMNS
LOVE AND DESPISES PASSION

FALSE love, sweet love, false love, thy prim-
    rose lands
Are bitten by a sea that gnaws and stains :
False love, thy river may have golden sands,
Yet rocks it sighing on thro' flinty plains.
The low continual forest hears of love :
The cloud-crest tells the under lake of him.
He wakes the plaint of rainbow-breasted
    dove,
The glowworm lights her torch, his herald
    dim,
The March wind is his furious trumpeter,
The cuckoo is his clear remembrancer.

Yet will I nothing of this herdsman Love,
This god of bread and cheese,
This paragon of ploughgirls: at mine ease,
Saint and serene above
Their trivial kisses, with the stars I write
The oracles of God,
Sown on the windy pinnacles of night.
My Life shall be
An Alpine morning o'er a tideless sea
Of avalanches bright.
As some peak never trod,
Rosy and pure in crystal ether set,
And from the world's foundation icebound yet:
Auroral, sweet, and inaccessible,
That rock shall be my sign.   The terrible
Hand of the Sun shall fall in harmless glows,
Nor melt one wreath of calm aërial snows ;
Not Titan's golden hour
Can melt my Danae tower:
Nor rain of richest beams
Unfreeze the frozen seams
Of ice and cloud, that veil me in my bower.

Fate gives me beauty, God has given me
    scorn.
I will be first or none :
To hew the wood of life I was not born ;
Flowers are my hands, my robe a tissue spun.
Shall I be jumbled up with market wives,
The herd and trash of maidens, who accept
Their long laborious lives,
Bewailing and bewept ?
And wear away their sordid household days,
Much as the steers, who pull the plough or
    graze.
I will not put my mouth up to some fool,
And be unvirgined for the kiss of him.
I will remain damsel of God, and rule
My worst thought purer than the morning
    rim.
I am locked up with God, and earthly yearn-
    ing,
In eyes as unresponsive to desire,
Passes, as puppets in a peepshow turning,
Gestures of painted passion, wood and wire.

What is this homespun comedy of Love,
Rank with the furrow-cleaving herdsman's
toil ?
What is this vineyard lodge, this red alcove,
Reed-roofed among the orchards of the oil ?
The floor is purple with the broken grape :
The vats are foamed with ferment. Hand
in hand,
Red to the knee, each Bacchanalian shape
Tramples the rich blood of the vineyard
land.
Or in some croft, half hid by rustic eaves,
The milkmaid rests her pail among the
leaves,
And the pied stirk with comfortable sound
Crops the abounding ground.
There, if some uncouth Thyrsis chance to
pass,
He comes and sits him by this freckled
lass,
And puts his brows to hers, this cow-girl
queen,

Coarse-grained and stained with summer, as
some green
Crude orchard apple, striped abrupt in
hue ;
And takes her rough hand fondly, where
the grass
Shoots up in timothies and ox-eyes too,
And the rathe sorrel, reddest of spring's
crew ;
And heaven finds echoes in the speedwell's
blue :
And pale green spikes are everywhere
around,
And chirping things give sound,
Hid in the ambush of the hay ; the quail
Is darnel-tangled, and the water-rail
Cheeps from the mere befringed with galin-
gale :
And mighty Pan breathes o'er the vernal
ground.
So deep in grass, as two hid meadow
birds,

They sing again their threadbare song,
  whose words
Are kisses : and in arrogance suppose
Their horny rushlight lantern can enclose
The radiant sun of demigod Desire.
What is this fen-fire, framed of mud and
  mire ?
Love, what is Love, the solace of the
  clown,
That makes the wise man frown ?
A ribbon in the milkmaid's frowsy hairs,
A few dog-roses in a field of tares,
A little laughter and a long disdain ;
Blind and unfit to reign,
The deity of pain ;
Silenus of the swineherds is his name,
The ploughboy Eros with his face of
  shame,
His woolly coat, his sheepdog at his side ;
Shall I unlock to such a mongrel god
The porches of my pride,
Or my serene abode ?

Throned on the cloud above such earthborn
    coil,
I rule by right of beauty such as toil.
I am the lily without fleck or soil.
Avaunt, thou son of mire,
No Tempe gave thee birth ;
Ether I am and fire.
I rise as flame, I rise,
Above this atmosphere of sighs
Beyond the reek of earth :
And Pythoness aspire,
Helmed with an angel's mirth :
Where star-dew steeps my beaming crest
    and hair,
Listening what cadence rare,
And on gross earth unheard,
The planets make in sphering. With what
    word
The morning star comes dripping back to
    God,
When he the sea at early morn has trod.
With what a beautiful clear even-song

Recurrent Vesper surges back among
The small pure rounded lights, which in the
    rain
Of light around him, pale and dumb, refrain
Their sparkling throng.
Shall I, whose meteor beauty makes the
    plain
Of the blue night mute with amazement,
    deign
To drop the corner of an eye at Love,
From golden spheres above?

Take my disdain, false Love, and hence
    begone,
Stained with rude wreck and clay;
Poor pipe of earthly passion, in whose
    tone
There only lives the discord of a day.
Leave me my isolation, grand and calm,
While fond adoring nations bend the knee,
Exclaiming, she is worthy of the palm,
As Dryad fair or mermaid of the sea.

Let their triumphant psalm
Acclaim me loveliest of the things that be.
Let them adore afar ;
And worship, as they please :
Love, if they choose ; but I am as the star
Out of the reach of these.

THE TRAGEDY OF CHILDHOOD

FAIREST leaves of autumn spread
To shroud with green these children dead ;
Their early fate, their cruel doom,
Might well require a nobler tomb :
Alabaster might explain,
Pompous verse rehearse their pain.
Cherubs weeping stony tears,
Time with scythe and Fate with shears,
Slab of lapis, jasper border,
Columns of Corinthian order ;
Let no meaner shrine be here
Than on the dust of cavalier.

Nay, they need no trophies high,
Grander in simplicity ;
And their oft-repeated tale
Is never old and never stale.
All night long in evil' case,
Thro' thorny green and forest space ;
Up and down, and far and wide,
They wandered till they sank and died.
Pitying on a hazel bough,
Robin saw them sinking low.
Came the wren, the whitethroat came,
Came the bird of evil name ;
Owl, and nuthatch, tit, and dove,
Singers of the dirge of love.
Will ye mourn them half as well
With the peal of muffled bell ?
With the organ march of Death,
With the floated incense wreath,
Chant and candle, cross and stole,
As the *misereres* roll ?
Here each tender baby lies
Shrined with richer obsequies :

Fairy leaves of aspen shed
Treasure round these children dead,
Leaves of oak, and sprays of rue,
Cypress branches, boughs of yew.
And they want no marble tomb,
Where we may inscribe their doom ;
Where the Frost with icy fetters
Tears away the golden letters.
Where the Rain rubs out the tale.
But their story shall not fail,
Shrined beyond the reach of chance
In golden childhood's first romance,
And on early Fancy's walls
Painted, where soft sunlight falls.

THE WINDMILL

Desolate windmill, eyelid of the distance,
　　Gaunt as a gibbet, ruled against the sky :
Rolling and rocking in the wind's persistence,
　　Thy black uplifted dome-house seems to
　　　　fly :

Writhing its wings, as eagle Promethean,
　　Who tears the Titan on Caucasian height.
While all the gentle gods above sing pæan,
　　To see Jove's red-winged vengeance rend
　　　　and smite.

Emblem of Life, whose roots are torn asunder,
　　An isolated soul that hates its kind,
Who loves the region of the rolling thunder,
　　And finds seclusion in the misty wind.

K　　　　　145

Type of a love, that wrecks itself to pieces
   Against the barriers of relentless Fate,
And tears its lovely pinions on the breezes
   Of just too early or of just too late.

The desolation of a moorland wasted,
   An endless heath, half-tinged with redden-
     ing ling :
Gray bitter tracts which ploughshare never
     tasted,
   Too sour to waken at the voice of spring.

These wiry roots revive not, when the
     zephyrs
   Unclasp the budded fragrance on the
     thorn.
Not here shall come the sound of lowing
     heifers,
   Not here shall heave the rippling waves
     of corn.

In thee, old mill, I see Ixion quiver,
  Chained on a wheel in Acherusian deep,
Upon whose weary eyelids not for ever
  Descends the healing balm of angel sleep.

I see some dragon-fly with wings outshadow
  The current-dancing midge, whose mur-
    mur fails
Beneath the swooping tyrant of the meadow,
  Bat-like and spectral, with loud latticed
    sails.

At eve thou loomest like a one-eyed giant
  To some poor crazy knight, who pricks
    along,
And sees thee wave in haze thy arms defiant,
  And growl the burden of thy grinding song.

Against thy russet sail-sheet slowly turning,
  The raven beats belated in the blast :
Behind thee ghastly, bloodred Eve is burning,
  Above, rose-feathered drifts are racking fast.

147

The curlews pipe around their plaintive dirges,
 Thou art a Pharos to the sea-mews hoar,
Set sheer above the tumult of the surges,
 As sea-mark on some spacious ocean floor.

My heart is sick with gazing on thy feature,
 Old blackened sugar-loaf with fourfold
  wings,
Thou seemest as some monstrous insect
  creature,
 Some mighty chafer armed with iron stings.

Emblem of man, who, after all his moaning,
 And strain of dire immeasurable strife,
Has yet this consolation, all atoning,—
 Life, as a windmill, grinds the bread of Life.

ROLAND AT RONCESVALLES

Roll up thy tardy legions, Charlemagne,
Haste to my succour : red in glory ride
The heaving furrows of the battle tide :
Advance, wipe out this pagan horde of Spain,
Whose rabble myriads crush me.   In disdain
Thy paladins, thy chivalry have died.
They sleep unbroken in their ranks of pride,
And where they nobly fought, lie nobly slain.

Farewell, my gallant bugle-horn, farewell,
Come, let me wind thy martial note once
    more,
And peal one last, one loud despairing cry ;
Until the long reverberations swell,
To rock my death-dirge on the echoing shore,
And all the Fontarabian woods reply.

149

THE ABSENT MARINER

SAILOR of the hoary deep,
   Thou art rolled from tide to tide.
I can watch the waves and weep :
   Thou canst roam the ocean wide.
I tremble at the rising gale,
Yet in the calm I chide thy sail :
For not one ship on all the main
Can bring my true-love home again.

Over realms of restless foam,
   Boundless breadths of heaving sea,
Rock, O wind, my rover home,
   Zephyr, blow his sails to me.
Waft him on thy tender wing,
Like the long-delaying spring :
Till, safe in port, with anchor cast,
He folds me in his arms at last.

Month on month, he sailed away,
   A speck upon the ocean line,
Melting in the rainy gray,
   Cloud-like on the utmost brine.
Autumn passed in discontent,
Winter came and winter went.
Day by day, I ponder dumb,
Spring is here—Ah! will he come?

A LAMENT

Yᴇ waves that sweep the splendid deep,
   And crest the ocean gray,
The voice of your eternal woe
Dilates in sorrow, to and fro,
   With pulse of broken spray.

Upraise thy dirge, thou furrowy surge,
   Whereon the stormlight glows,
Rock on the shining island side,
And break with foam the crimson pride
   Of the half-opened rose.

From the grave gate a gust of Fate
   Blew stern at Death's decree ;
And underneath its icy power
Lies withered, cold, the loveliest flower,
   That used to comfort me.

HODGE PROLOGIZES AT HIS PUBLIC

SCENE: A VILLAGE ALEHOUSE, NEAR A CHURCH SURROUNDED
BY A CHURCHYARD.   A WINDMILL TURNING
IN THE DISTANCE.

Sun and shine,
And ivy twine,
Thirst is bad on a midsummer day.
Sell thy flail
For a stoup of ale,
Shear thy lamb for a wisp of hay.

All over the church
The little birds perch,
And the graveyard is full as it well can be:
Headstone and mound,
And garden-like ground,
And plenty to pay for the vicar's fee.

153

A buttermilk wench,
And an alehouse bench,
With plenty to drink and a little to see ;
With a song and a pipe,
Till we 're reeling ripe,
And let the blue ribbon go hang for me.

Sun and shine,
And ivy twine,
Honey is best from a mountain bee.
The old black swift,
He lives in a rift
Under a beam of the church roof-tree.

By the churchyard rail
Is the house of ale,
Settle and mugs and a sanded floor.
A trough, where a sign
(I wish it were mine)
Creaks in the winds like a rusty door.

The sexton is nigh,
And his work is dry;
And the chink of a glass is as good as a bell,
To draw him inside
And be quickly supplied,
For he digs all the better for drinking a spell.

Sleet and hail
On the windmill sail;
Nobody grudges the rats their flour.
The mills of time
Grind girls in prime:
The wheels go round and the maid grows sour.

The red robin comes
To pick up the crumbs.
The wagtail runs nodding all over the lea.
A gun for a bird,
And a blow for a word,
And a measureless score at the Chequers for
me.

155

So my song it may pass,
If you'll stand us a glass
To the Church and the Queen: and plenty
to eat,
Oceans of drink,
And never to think,
And a good stiff tax on the foreigners' wheat.

THE WINE OF LIFE

HE best can drink the wine of Life,
  And sweetly crush the grape of Fate,
Who shuts the Janus doors of strife,
  And binds an olive on his gate.

Who needs no victim to atone
  The record of his blameless hour;
Contentment is the corner stone
  On which he builds his arch of power.

He best enjoys who can refrain,
  He least is nimble Fortune's fool,
Who sees his honest Duty plain,
  A scholar in her iron school.

How idle for a spurious fame
　To roll in thorn-beds of unrest :
What matter whom the mob acclaim,
　If thou art master of thy breast ?

If sick thy soul with fear and doubt,
　And weary with the rabble din,—
If thou wouldst scorn the herd without,
　First make the discord calm within.

If we are lords in our disdain,
　And rule our kingdoms of despair,
As fools we shall not plough the main
　For halters made of syren's hair.

We need not traverse foreign earth
　To seek an alien Sorrow's face.
She sits within thy central hearth,
　And at thy table has her place.

So with this hour of push and pelf,
　Where nought unsordid seems to last,
Vex not thy miserable self,
　But search the fallows of the past.

In Time's rich tract behind us lies
  A soil replete with root and seed ;
There harvest wheat repays the wise,
  While idiots find but charlock weed.

There we can hear the flute of Pan,
  Bewailing down the reedy vales:
There see the tempest-beaten swan
  Sail broken, down the moaning gales.

And larger heroes in that morn
  Stride mist-like thro' the asphodel,
And hoary bards with cheeks unshorn
  Invoke anew the lyric spell.

On me their burning helms they turn,
  Their eagle banners awe the glen,
They, rising from each dusty urn,
  Display their giant limbs again.

A broad cup brimmed with mighty red
  These silent years to us assign ;
From old Falernian vineyards shed,
  The Roman sends the Teuton wine.

159

Old Fauns have breathed against the grapes,
    Old-world aromas haunt the bowl ;
Still music of forgotten shapes,
    Dim pathos of a Pagan soul.

There from those dark and glimmering lands,
    From altars wrecked with ivy trail,
Old Flaccus reaches out his hands,
    And bids the mild barbarian hail.

www.ingramcontent.com/pod-product-compliance
Lightning Source LLC
Chambersburg PA
CBHW020012030726
47500CB00002B/545